# MYSTERIOUS MONSTERS

# BOOK 2:

# ALIEN

COMING TO A BASEMENT NEAR YOU

Mysterious Monsters: Alien

For more information, to inquire about rights to this or other works, or to purchase copies for special educational, business, or sales promotional uses please write to:

Corgi Bits is an imprint of Incorgnito Publishing Press
A division of Market Management Group, LLC
300 E. Bellevue Drive, Suite 208
Pasadena, California 91101

FIRST EDITION

Printed in the United States of America

ISBN:    978-1-944589-23-3

10 9 8 7 6 5 4 3 2 1

*For Mike and Mary Blanchard*

# Contents

# INTRODUCTION

# ALIEN

Dear Readers,

Please think carefully about whether you wish to read this book. If you have not yet met the Mattigans — Maddie (12), Max (10) and Theo (8) — be warned: they might be a little too *out there* for you. They're not exactly normal kids.

Unless you think it's *normal* to go looking for monsters.

But it's not just that they go looking for monsters. They've actually *found* one — a five-hundred-pound Sasquatch. And it's not just that they actually found a Sasquatch. It's that they're hiding him in the basement of their rickety old mansion on the edge of Portland's Forest Park.

Question: What would *you* do if you discovered that Mysterious Monsters were real when your father is the star of "Monstrous Lies with Marcus Mattigan," a TV show dedicated to proving they aren't?

If your answer is, tell your dad and deal with the consequences, you should *definitely* find another book. I recommend "One Upon a Time Good Children Made Good Choices and Lived Happily Ever After." It's a good one.

Still here?

I guess that means you're willing to go along for the ride, wherever it takes you. Which is perfect, because when you're ready, you will find the Mattigan kids with their famous father heading out on a road trip to Vegas, betting that they can get control of this rather hairy situation on their own.

Perhaps you already know that in Vegas, most bets don't turn out very well.

Maybe you also know that there's a rule people have when they travel to the City of Lights: "What happens in Vegas *stays* in Vegas."

Well, lucky for you, brave reader — this time it doesn't.

CHAPTER ONE

# ROAD SIGNS

"Dad," Maddie said as gently as she could, "you've barely said a word this entire trip. Don't you think we should talk about what we're going to do once we get to the hotel?"

Marcus looked at his daughter from behind the wheel of the "Yuck," the Mattigan's lovable, but beat-up old truck. He seemed almost surprised to find her next to him, then to see his two boys in the rearview mirror. He'd been in a semi-trance for pretty much the entire two days they'd been on the road. The trip was dragging on forever — even allowing for the fact that they had to drive cautiously towing their Fifth Wheel camper. Every time Maddie mentioned how slowly he was driving, her father sped up, but only for about five minutes. Then he went back to puttering again.

"I'm really sorry," Marcus finally said. "I get this way before my investigations. I go over every possible scenario I can think of in my head. This time I'm feeling a little extra pressure, because I, perhaps unwisely, sent out a press release."

"So, you figured out how to catch the alien then, Dad? Over."

"Theo!" Max objected. "Dad's not going to *catch* the alien! He's a *professional skeptic.* He's going to prove there *is no alien!* Over!"

Even though Max and Theo were sitting shoulder-to-shoulder on the Yuck's back bench, they were talking to each other on Max's spy walkie-talkies.

"You know what I meant!" Theo claimed. "Over!"

"No, we didn't," Maddie informed him. What she wanted to add — but of course didn't — was *that she and her brothers were going to catch the alien all by themselves.* Instead she said, "We're sorry that video of us looking for Bigfoot damaged your reputation, Dad.

I know that's why you put out a press release. We're sure you'll figure out what's really going on in Vegas — and your show will be back on the air right away."

"Like you always say," Max put in, "if there's one natural resource the world will never run out of, it's phonies, fakes and fraudsters!"

"True story," Marcus said, and he smiled.

*"People,"* the Yuck full of Mattigans sighed.

*"Sooo,"* Maddie said, feeling a rather uncomfortable sensation in the pit of her stomach, an ache she got whenever she was sorta-kinda not exactly telling the whole truth. "What exactly *is* going on in Vegas with this alien escape story?"

"For the last fifty years or so," Marcus replied, sounding finally ready to talk, "people have believed — people who believe unbelievable things, that is — that the military has been hiding downed UFOs at their formerly secret base a hundred miles north of Las Vegas."

"Area 51," Maddie said. She hadn't wanted to

bug her father for information while he seemed so, well, *spacey.* So she'd spent their driving time so far reading as much as she could about aliens on her phone. She now knew all about how Area 51 supposedly housed the UFOs that crashed near Roswell, New Mexico, in 1947, and in Kingman, Arizona, in 1953 — not to mention other sites.

"Right," Marcus confirmed. "And they supposedly captured the aliens that were onboard some of those crafts." He glanced at his daughter to see what she thought of this. *"Alive,"* he added. "One of them is even supposed to have been working for the government all these years at Area 51. J-Rod they call him. He's the one who the Internet says has escaped and is running around the desert, hiding from the authorities — not to mention the who-knows-how-many UFO buffs out there, trying to catch him first."

When Marcus saw only wonder in his daughter's big, brown eyes, he looked at his boys in the rearview mirror again. They looked back at him with outright amazement.

Marcus waited some more, glancing from one of his kids to the next with increasing concern.

Finally, they caught on.

*"People!"* the kids all sighed together again — this time, extra loud.

Marcus shook his head, clearly relieved to be agreeing with his kids about the foolishness of fools who believed in little green men, especially the kind of foolish fools who believed the government was hiding them.

Absurd!

Maddie shot a quick glance back at her brothers. She Eyeballed them big time, and they understood what she meant: They'd better be careful or their father would realize they'd changed their minds about the existence of unproven things like little green men — especially now that he'd finally started talking. They needed to get him to tell them his plan, so they could make *their*s. Whisper-arguing under their covers last night in the Fifth Wheel about whether aliens actually *were* little green men had been a total waste of time.

"Are they saying how this J-Rod supposedly escaped?" Max asked, shoving his phone back into his pocket. He'd spent his driving time reading websites on how to improve his observational skills, which he knew were a spy's greatest asset. They all said that every little thing mattered. Every word. Every detail.

"No one seems to know how the rumor started," Marcus explained. "But that's where I come in. I'm going to trace it to its source, and then I'm going to prove it's all a bunch of balderdash."

Theo had spent his driving time on his phone as well, watching a movie called "Harry and the Hendersons." "But what if it's not a bunch of *dalderbash?*" he asked. "What if the alien is real, and your dad was right the whole time about Mysterious Monsters — even though he should have never abandoned you when you were just a kid to go looking for them, like we're doing?"

"Theo!"

*"What, Maddie?"*

16

"We're not looking for Mysterious Monsters!"

"You know what I mean!"

"No, Theo, we don't," Max told him, and not kindly.

"Is something wrong with you guys?" Marcus asked.

"All good," the three kids grumbled.

"It's getting late, and I think you've been cooped up in here too long," Marcus concluded. "You all probably need more space."

No one said anything to this.

"More *space,*" Marcus repeated. "See what I did there? Or is my humor too *alien* for you?"

"Is there a barf bag in here?" Max asked.

"I do have a sick sense of humor," Marcus joked. "Fortunately, I think we're just about there."

They were leaving the highway, at last.

"*Anyway,* Dad," Maddie said. "How exactly are you planning to trace the source of the escape rumor?"

"Well — "

"Look at that!" Theo blurted. They'd stopped at a red light at the end of the exit ramp.

*"What now?"* Maddie sighed.

"There!" Theo said, pointing.

On the shoulder of the road, a tumbleweed was blowing by. Remarkably, it looked very much like a flying saucer.

"It's a sign!" Theo cried.

"It's not a sign," Maddie said as they headed into the city streets. "Dad, your plan? Area 51?"

"Oh, well," he said. "You really don't need to worry about it. It's not like I'm going to try to break into the highest-security military facility in the world. I'm just going to poke around town, make some calls — see who will talk to me. You guys can have fun at the hotel. Very kid-friendly these days."

"But" — Max objected — "we want to help with the detective work!"

"Max, you're ten years old," Marcus pointed out.

"At least tell us what you're thinking," Maddie urged. "We do have good ideas."

"Well — "

"Haaa!" Theo howled. "Ha-ha-ha!" He banged on the window next to him, but also pointed again. He was laughing too hard to speak. *"Ah*-ha-ha-ha!"

*"Now what?"* Maddie cried.

"Sign!" Theo finally managed to choke.

"I told you, a stupid tumbleweed is not a sign!"

"But *that* is!" Theo spluttered. "At that gas station. 'EAT HERE, GET GAS FREE!' *Ha-ha-ha-ha-ha!"*

"Theo, *please,*" Maddie begged, seeing what he was pointing to now. "Max, make him stop already!" She glared at him. They needed to hear their father's plan!

Max looked at Maddie. He looked at Theo, then back at Maddie. Then he couldn't hold it in anymore. *"Bah-ha-ha!"* he wailed.

"Forget them," Maddie said, turning back to face

front. "Dad, you can just tell *me* the plan. *Dad?*"

"Har-har-har!"

*"Dad!"*

CHAPTER TWO

# LITTLE GREEN MOB SCENE

"Wow!" the Mattigan kids cried, immediately forgetting what they were all fussing about. The Yuck had turned a corner, and there it was, spread out before them in all its glittering glory: the famous Las Vegas Strip.

It had been dark for a while by then, so everything was lit up like Christmas, times ten. They'd seen it in pictures, of course — in the movies too — but it was different in real life. It was bigger and brighter, more gleaming and glowing.

It was like they'd entered another world.

Neon World.

Marcus drove around so they could see the most

famous sites: the mini-Eiffel tower at the Paris; the New York skyline at New York - New York; the giant Pyramid of the Luxor, which seemed to have fallen out of a portal in the sky; even the Stratosphere, with the roller coaster perched on top.

All three Mattigan kids let out *oohs* and *ahhs* along the way, right up to the moment they arrived at their destination: The Circus Circus, and its giant, blacktopped parking lot.

Once they finally found a parking spot, Marcus turned to everyone and said, "Here's the plan, gang. It's already past eleven, so it's straight to bed for everybody. Tomorrow, at nine a.m. sharp, I'll start calling around to set up some meetings with military folks. I think — given that I'm trying to help prove these monster rumors are false — they'll be more than happy to speak with me. Two local filmmakers will meet us here — both are good friends. One, Kirk, will go out with me. The other, Nyota, will do some interviewing at the casino. I will buy an all-day pass for you guys to play at the Adventure Dome Theme Park and the Midway, but you'll check in with Nyota every hour. I'll make sure you have her cell number."

"Awesome!" Theo cried. "And we get to sleep in the hotel, right?"

"You didn't think we would drive all the way to Vegas to sleep in the Fifth Wheel, did you?" Marcus asked.

"No way!"

"But you can if you really want to."

"No way!"

"All right, then," Marcus said as he climbed out of the Yuck. "You drive a hard bargain."

Max and Maddie waited until their father went to start unloading their bags. Then they let their little brother have it.

"Dad's plan is *not* awesome, Theo!" Maddie whisper-shouted. "His plan means *we* have no plan! This is not good."

"You knew what I meant!"

"No, we didn't!" Max snapped.

"Kids?"

The kids hurried to join their father, who already had their stuff waiting for them. Everyone shouldered their bags. Then they headed through the lot toward the casino, falling in with a large number of other people.

"Boy, it's crowded here!" Theo said. "Is it always this crowded here, Dad?"

"Pretty much," Marcus said. "But especially for special events."

*Like alien hunting,* the kids all thought.

"So, who is your friend going to interview at the casino?" Max asked, using his innocent spy voice. Maddie nodded at him to show it was an observant question that might get their father talking again.

"Oh," Marcus said, apparently not hearing the question. "Speaking of special events, I booked us here because — "

"Hey, look at that!"

"Enough already, Theo!" Maddie cried.

"No, look!"

Everyone looked.

Theo was pointing at someone, or some*thing*, in the crowd as they walked through it. "A little green man!"

Sure enough, someone was dressed up — though not very well — like the typical little-green-man alien. The oversized green head looked totally fake, and you could see his face right through the eyeholes.

"And look at that!"

Closer to the doors, was a second little green man in a much more impressive costume.

*"Look at that!"*

This time, no one needed to ask what Theo was talking about.

They'd entered the casino, and they all saw what he saw: milling about the reception area were hundreds of little green men.

It was a little green mob scene.

# CHAPTER THREE

# ET-CON

It turned out that they weren't actually *all* little green men. There were also little green women. Big ones, too — men and women. Not all of them were green, now that the Mattigans got a better look at them. Some were blue, some were red, some had antennas. Some had three or more eyes, some of which were on stalks. There were extra arms, too — and extra teeth. But they were all attached to aliens, and the aliens were everywhere, all holding funny-colored drinks in strangely shaped glasses and chattering away like they were at some sort of interstellar cocktail party.

One alien seemed to be in charge. He was of medium height and wore, like a number of the others, a large grey mask that showed off big almond-shaped eyes, nostrils but no real nose, and a thin slit of a mouth. His fancy-looking red robe swayed behind him as he moved around greeting new arrivals. "Welcome!" he boomed after shaking each new three- or four- or six-fingered hand. "Welcome to Planet Earth on behalf of Alien Nation!"

"What the heck is going on?" Maddie asked her brothers. Their father had hurried over to the check-in desk, where he'd spotted an opening. "Is this one of those weird grown-up theme parties? Is this why they say, 'what happens in Vegas stays in Vegas?' I wouldn't want anyone at home to know this is what I was doing here. Totally embarrassing."

"Look!"

"For crying out loud already, Theo! Oh — sorry."

Theo was pointing to a large banner that read, "WELCOME TO THE FIRST ANNUAL ET-CON."

"What does that mean?" Maddie asked.

"Must be a convention," Max guessed. "Like Comic-Con, but about ET's. Extra-terrestrials. Looks like it officially starts tomorrow and goes through the weekend."

"Okay, but what *is* it?"

"Well, they'd have presentations from experts, and panel discussions, maybe shows and sales, lots of sales — of things people made, of anything related to aliens: from t-shirts to alien language books to 'authentic moon rocks' to — *whatever.*"

"I want a tumbleweed shaped like a flying saucer," Theo said.

"This is why Dad booked us here," Maddie realized.

"And I think we have a pretty good idea of who Dad wants his friend to interview tomorrow," Max said, gesturing at the mingling aliens. "Perfect background material for 'Monstrous Lies with Marcus Mattigan.'"

Maddie thought about this for a moment. "Guess what else we have," she said.

"What?" her brothers asked.

"A plan."

# CHAPTER FOUR

# THE PLAN, PART I

The next morning, Maddie climbed out from under her covers on the couch that she'd been stuck with and tiptoed to the queen bed just a few feet away.

*"Max,"* she whispered, shaking him by the shoulder. It was 8 a.m., but the hotel room was still dark because of the blackout curtains. Her thicket of hair was morning wild. Her brothers' Mattigan Messes — Theo's curls and Max's shaggy mop — spilled all over their pillows.

*"Hrmmm,"* Max murmured.

*"This is your first spy-signment!"*

Max bolted upright. Theo grumbled next to him, but did not wake up. Marcus grunted like Bigfoot in the other bed, but he didn't wake up, either.

Maddie sighed as Max snuck into the bathroom to get dressed. When he came out, he got down on the floor and pulled his spy kit out from under the bed. It was his dad's old briefcase. Now, it held Max's *spy-nocular*, a cheap, motion-sensor alarm system, his *spy-nifying* glass, a Swiss Army knife, a stethoscope, and an invisible-ink pen and decoder. While her brother prepared his spy supplies, Maddie slipped her father's keys off the dresser.

Then Max and Maddie snuck out of the room and silently rode the elevator down to the lobby. They headed toward the casino's front entrance, but along the way they both got distracted by the buzzing and plinging and ringing all around them.

Lights blinked. Video screens flashed. There were groans and cheers from all directions.

People were sitting at machines tapping buttons. They were sitting at tables rolling dice and holding cards and moving chips. Max and Maddie stood there, turning slowly in circles, taking it all in. The ET-Con party had distracted them last night. They'd been too tired to notice the spectacle of gambling.

"Who *are* these people?" brother and sister asked each other at exactly the same time.

They stood and watched some more, mesmerized. Something was seriously wrong with this scene.

*"They* look like aliens," Max said, after observing a blank-faced old lady tap the same button on a slot machine about 200 hundred straight times, without moving a single other part of her body. "Actually, not aliens: *zombies. "*

"Is this what happens when you gamble?" Maddie wondered aloud. "Is *this* why they say 'what happens in Vegas stays in Vegas'?"

"Hey, there, you two!" someone called, startling the kids. It was an enthusiastic someone with a very pleasant voice. Max and Maddie looked away from the zombies to see a rosy-cheeked woman smiling at them. She had attractive blue eyes and the whitest teeth they'd ever seen. On her very fancy dress was a nametag that said, "Hostess."

"Hi!" both Max and Maddie said back. Neither of them ever spoke in such a chipper tone. Something about this woman just brought it out of them.

"You two look like you might enjoy two free ten-dollar cards for the Fun Zone!" the woman said. "Whaddaya say? It's right there." She pointed to a large, open enclosure just beyond the zombies. "Want to take a peek?" she asked. "No strings attached. Totally free!"

"Well, okay, I guess," Maddie said. "We'll just have a quick look." And before they knew it, she and Max were following the charming lady across the lobby and into the Fun Zone.

*"Ta-da!"* the hostess said, opening her arms wide so they could take in all the new flashing and beeping and video noise.

It was overwhelming, and Max and Maddie both sensed that something, once again, wasn't right.

"Beautiful, isn't it?" the lady asked. "Like a dream world, where you can get away from it all."

"Wait a minute," Max said. "Where are all the actual games?"

"What do you mean?" the lady asked, smiling at him with a smile so large he thought her pretty face might fall off. "It's wall-to-wall games in here!"

"These aren't games," Maddie said, seeing what her brother saw now. "Look, in that one, you just hope the wheel stops on your color. It's exactly like roulette. Which is gambling. And in that one, you drop a token in, just *hoping* others will fall off the shelf and give you more tokens. So you can just put them back in and hope to win more. Where are the arcade games — where you actually get to play something? These — these are — "

"For training kids how to be zombies when they grow up," Max said. "They give you the free card to lure you in."

The lady's smile was gone now. Her friendly face had vanished. *"You aren't normal children,"* she hissed.

"True story."

"Hey, there, you two!" the lady called, smiling wide again. She'd spotted another pair of kids and headed right for them.

"Let's get out of here," Max said.

"Right!" Maddie agreed. "What were we doing, anyway?"

After shaking themselves out of their daze, Max and Maddie rushed out of the Fun Zone and then right out of the casino. They hurried through the parking lot to the Yuck.

*"Um —* " Max said as his sister looked to see if anyone was watching — no one was — and then quickly unlocked the rear door of the Fifth Wheel for him.

"No," Maddie said, reading her brother's mind, "in Nevada you cannot be back here while the Yuck is moving. But in Oregon — Dad's been wrong about this — it turns out you *are* allowed, *if* there is communication possible with the driver. I looked it all up last night on my phone."

"But — "

"Hold on."

Maddie dove into the Yuck, then emerged with one of Max's walkie-talkies. "Here," she said. "The other one's under Dad's seat. If there's an emergency, use it. We have Oregon plates, so I'm sure that if Dad gets pulled over, and they find you in the camper, they'll understand — if you say we all thought the laws were the same."

"What's wrong?"

Maddie Eyeballed Max. "Nothing, what's wrong with you?"

"It's just — "

"It's the best we can do, Max. Do you have a better idea?"

"No, it's just — "

"What? It's just what?"

"It's just that Dad's always saying the world's full of fakers and fraudsters. Aren't we — ?"

*"Look,"* Maddie sighed. She was doing an awful

36

lot of sighing on this trip. "I don't feel great about it, either, but think about it this way: Why do liars and cheaters lie and cheat?"

"To get things they didn't earn."

"Exactly. Is that what we're doing?"

"No. Not at all."

"It matters *why* you do what you do. I'm sure the best spies have to cut some corners, every once in a while, to catch the worst criminals. You can't make an omelet if you don't break a few eggs."

"Teachable Moment?"

"Teachable Moment."

"That's pretty good," Max admitted. "You'd make a pretty good spy, and a pretty good breakfast, too."

"Thank you. But please know that if anything happens to you, I will never, ever forgive myself. Your spy assignment is just that: *spy.* Find out where Dad goes, who he meets, what he does, and what he finds out. Text me in real time. Come back in one piece.

That's it. Got it? What are you doing?"

"Getting into my spy crouch."

"I guess you're ready, then. In you go."

Maddie opened the door to the Fifth Wheel and Max crouched inside. She Eyeballed him a good one, just in case — even though he wasn't looking — then locked him in tight. Then she let out a major-league sigh.

After that, ignoring her aching stomach, she high-tailed it back to the casino.

CHAPTER FIVE

# THE PLAN, PART II

Maddie had just finished stuffing the extra pillows under Max's side of the covers when her father sat up in his bed. His Mattigan Mess looked like electricity had shocked it.

*"You're up already?"* he whispered when he saw Maddie standing there with a hand on her gut.

*"Uh, yeah,"* she whispered back. It was 8:25 a.m. She'd been planning to wake her dad in four minutes, exactly one minute before he normally got up in order to hit the ground running at nine.

"Are you not feeling well? Why do you have my keys?"

Maddie had forgotten to put them back on the dress-

39

er. Those zombies down in the casino had really thrown her off — and that creepy Fun Zone lady, too. And her "omelet" of fibs was making her feel like throwing up.

"Because," she stuttered, "I — I saw you starting to wake up a few minutes ago, and — and I think we need to sleep in — after all that driving. Your keys fell on the floor, and I didn't want you to have to search around for them and accidentally wake the boys."

*"Oh, okay,"* Marcus whispered. He climbed out of bed and took the keys. "That's very thoughtful of you," he added. "I'll get dressed quietly and go grab some breakfast in the camper."

When he slipped into the bathroom, Maddie quickly texted Max a warning, then climbed back into her couch, hoping her father wouldn't want to kiss them good-bye before he left.

Marcus came out just two minutes later and approached the boys' bed. He was definitely going to kiss them good-bye.

Maddie held her breath. She didn't know what to do.

Then she heard her brother mutter something from under his covers. It sounded like, *"Histafistafoo!"*

"Oh!" Maddie said, after a moment of total confusion. She sat up and whisper-shouted, *"Notta foot, notta fist, notta finger!"* Her father was just starting to lean over the lump that wasn't Max. "We'll get along fine, Dad," she promised. "Don't wake them up. Good luck out there."

"Oklahoma," Marcus agreed, straightening up. "Make sure you touch base with Nyota before you leave the room. Her cell number is on the dresser. I'll be in touch."

And then he left.

Or, he almost left.

He had his hand on the doorknob when Maddie said, "Dad?"

"Yes?"

"Can I ask you something?"

"Sure." Marcus came back into the room a few steps.

"I know this will sound crazy," she said, stalling to make sure that Max had gotten himself hidden, but also because she was suddenly curious. "But just humor me, okay?"

"Okay."

"Remember how you said you wouldn't want to know if any of the creatures in that monster journal were real?"

"Maddie, I threw that collection of nonsense away as soon as — "

"Remember how you said you wouldn't want to know if any of them were real, because you wouldn't want to change how you feel about your dad abandoning you as a kid to search for Mysterious Monsters?"

"Sigh," Marcus said. "Don't tell me you're starting to believe this silliness about an alien running around out there in the desert."

"No — of course not," Maddie promised. "I'm only asking. I'm just saying — if it were true, would you want to know about it?"

42

Marcus seemed to think about the question seriously for a moment. Then he said, "If you're asking me, would I want to know if the entire world turned upside down and nothing made sense anymore? I'd guess I'd have to say, 'thank you very much, but no.'"

"Because of your dad?"

"Yes," Marcus admitted. "But also because of your mom."

*"Mom?"* Maddie gasped, her heart racing. They almost never talked about her mom anymore. They'd stopped about six months after her disappearance, which was a whole year ago. It just hurt too much.

"If nothing makes sense anymore — if there are no rules — then I'll never learn what happened to her."

"Okay, then," Maddie said, holding back a giant sob. "We won't tell you when we find the alien."

"Much appreciated," Marcus said. His frown flipped to a smile, which made Maddie smile, too, if only for a moment.

Her father slipped out of the room.

Theo sat up when the door clicked shut. "That was a close one!" he said.

"Too close for comfort, that's for sure," Maddie agreed, holding her stomach.

## CHAPTER SIX

# FIFTH WHEEL, PART I

Max was looking around the Fifth Wheel, transforming it into a secret spy headquarters in his mind, when his phone buzzed. It was a text from Maddie.

*d coming 2 5 w! hide!*

Quickly, but calmly, Max hustled into one of the camper's many little closets, the one with the "Monstrous Lies with Marcus Mattigan" TV show poster on it. Less than ten minutes later, he heard his dad climb inside.

A few moments after that, there was a knock on the Fifth Wheel's door, which Marcus opened.

"Kirk!" Max heard his father say. "Glad you could make it! Come on in. I was just going to wolf down some cereal, but it's early. How about joining me for an omelet?"

"Sure," the other man said. "Great to see you, Marcus."

Fanning himself in the hot little closet, Max listened to the men talk about the TV business while Marcus cooked up their breakfast. When they were done eating it, Marcus said, "Let's film the call to the Air Force Base. I'm sure they're getting flooded with reports of alien sightings, and I won't get through. But you never know."

There was a pause, and then Kirk said, "Rolling."

"Voicemail," Max heard his father grumble. Then, sounding more official, he said, "Hello, my name is Marcus Mattigan, host of 'Monstrous Lies with Marcus Mattigan.' I hope you know my work. Please disregard the recent Internet nonsense about me having my children wandering the woods of Oregon looking for Bigfoot. That was a set-up, a poor attempt at revenge by a fraud I exposed on an episode of my show. Which brings me to why I'm calling…"

Then he explained that he was in town to put an end to all the alien-escape rumors and left his number.

"Well," Marcus said, apparently done with the call, "let's head out to the base and see if anyone there will talk to us in person."

"Sounds good."

The two men climbed out of the Fifth Wheel, and moments later, the Yuck started up. Drenched in sweat, sucking in air, Max fell out of the closet. He hadn't realized he'd been holding his breath so much in there. His phone was in his hand, but he hadn't even thought of using it as a recording device.

He lay on his back, ashamed of himself.

*Some spy!*

## CHAPTER SEVEN

# WHEN IN OUTER SPACE

"This is the best I could do on short notice," Maddie said, emptying a grocery bag onto the bed. Theo had fallen back asleep, so Maddie went down to the lobby again to do some shopping. She'd been afraid even to look at the zombies, so she'd sprinted right past them to the casino shops.

"What's going on?" Theo muttered, sitting up and rubbing his eyes at the sudden light in the room. When he realized he was rubbing his eyes with *Mei-mei,* his old baby blanket, he quickly shoved it under his pillow. No one knew he'd brought it. No one even knew he still *had* it. Luckily, Maddie was looking through all the junk she'd just dumped on him. "What *is* all this stuff?" he asked.

There were some dorky sheets with spaceships on them, a bunch of make-up, hair bands, a roll of tinfoil, some weird sunglasses, and colored hairspray.

"I also bought some peanut-butter-and-banana-sandwich fixings for you," Maddie said. "And I called Nyota. She's going to meet us downstairs, but we need to hurry. The conference starts at ten, and I've already picked out our first session."

She waved some sort of program at Theo, who slouched at the thought of sitting through classes instead of riding roller coasters and playing games.

"I just hope we can get in without badges, or passes, or whatever."

"We're gonna sneak in?"

"I asked if there were still spots open, but it costs three hundred dollars to register for the conference."

"So we're gonna sneak in?"

Maddie sighed yet again. "I'm sorry, Theo," she said. "This conference is a great opportunity to learn about the whole alien *thing.* I just can't think of any other way to get us in. I don't want you to think sneaking into things is okay, but sometimes, if you want to make an omelet you have to — "

"Awesome!"

"Oh. I should have known."

"So what's all this junk for?"

"Teachable Moment," Maddie said: "When in Rome, do as the Romans do."

"What?"

"Okay, when in Las Vegas, do as the Las Vegas-ites? Do."

"I have no idea what you're talking about."

"Okay, try this one: 'When in outer space, do as the aliens do.'"

"I just woke up, Maddie!"

"Crikey, Theo! Everyone's dressed up like aliens down there! They say, "it takes a thief to catch a thief." Well, to catch aliens, you probably need some aliens. Time to get our outer space on!"

## CHAPTER EIGHT

# THE CALL

Max rushed over to one of the Fifth Wheel's seats and sat down, wondering what to do and where they were going. He popped open his spy kit to see if anything in there might be of use.

Just then he heard a phone ring. Panicking, he grabbed at his cell, but he quickly saw it wasn't ringing.

How could that be?

Then Max heard Kirk say, "Camera's rolling. Put the call on speaker."

How could *that* be?

Finally, Max finally realized what was happening.

"Check," Marcus told Kirk. Then he said, "Hello?"

Max texted Maddie.

*walkie talkie ON in yuck! u r a genius!*

A reply came right back.

*true story. just keep ur spy ears open.*

"Mr. Mattigan?" said a new voice on Max's walkie-talkie, coming from Marcus's cell phone in the Yuck. "Is this Mr. Marcus Mattigan, the professional skeptic?"

"Speaking," Marcus replied.

"This is Colonel Mike Blanchard of the United States Department of Homeland Security."

"Yes, wonderful! Thank you for returning my call so quickly."

"Oh — well, of course. Absolutely."

"I am happy to help end all these silly rumors, if you think there's something I can do."

"I believe there is, Mr. Mattigan," said this Colonel Mike Blanchard. "As you may know, hundreds of UFO fanatics are pouring into the area around Groom Lake. They're wandering through the desert, looking for this ridiculous J-Rod alien thing. We think the rumors are being encouraged by performers in costumes popping up here and there, mostly at night — you know, just to feed the frenzy. These people are putting themselves in harm's way and endangering our work in the process. We do important work here. Secret, but important."

"I understand."

"Do you have a GPS and a vehicle that can go off-road?"

"Yes, both."

"Outstanding. I have the email from your press release. I'm going to send you some coordinates. You'll no doubt note that they do not lead to the site everyone knows as 'Area 51.' Do not let that disturb you. It'll take you about an hour."

"I'll be there directly, Colonel Blanchard."

"Outstanding."

There was a click, after which Marcus said, *"In-nnteresting.* Verrry *innnteresting."*

With his heart pounding, Max tapped his phone again:

*going to area 51! the REAL area 51!!!!*

CHAPTER NINE

# SESSION A-1

Two aliens holding hands, both with green faces, sporting silver antennae and wrapped in spaceship bed sheets, headed through the Circus Circus lobby.

"Stop!" a man called.

They froze.

*"Crikey,"* Maddie said under her breath. *"They're on to us already."*

Brother and sister turned to see a man wearing jeans and a sports coat rushing their way.

*"She* made me do it!"

"Theo!"

"Adorable!" the man gushed. "You kids are absolutely *adorable!* Would you consider letting us film you for promotions?" Another man holding a video camera suddenly appeared next to him.

"Will we be famous?" Theo asked.

"Maybe!" the first man promised, grinning from ear-to-ear. "People all over the country — all over the world even — will see you! Our ads often go viral!"

"Oklahoma!"

"Well, there, too, I suppose!"

*"Hmmm,"* Maddie said. She didn't like the way this guy was talking to them, like they were babies. Or stupid. Or stupid babies. And his smile was too much like the Fun Zone lady's not to make her suspicious. "I assume you need our dad to sign a waiver," she said. "Unfortunately, he's out for the morning."

"Oh, well," the man said after a moment's pause. "That's actually not a problem. Since your faces won't be recognizable, it's totally cool."

"But if no one signs anything," Maddie pressed, "then I guess we won't get paid for being so adorable that we help advertise your business."

"Well, no. But remember you might go — "

"Viral. Right. Been there. Done that. We'll pass."

"*Humpf*!" Theo protested.

*"Those,"* the man said, drifting away with his partner, "are not normal children."

*"Those,"* someone else said, walking up to them, "are *brilliant* children." It was another person holding a video camera, a lovely Asian woman wearing a jacket with a million pockets on it. "Hi, Mattigans," she said. "I'm Nyota. I guessed it was you, though the costumes threw me off. I seriously advise you *not* to get filmed in them after your Bigfoot video — for your father's sake."

"Hi!" Maddie said. "It's nice to meet you. And you're right!" she realized, clutching her stomach again. "I didn't even think of that! It's just that, we were hoping to, well, sneak into one of the sessions — the one in Ballroom A — to learn about all this alien stuff. To *help* Dad."

"No worries. It's cool," Nyota said. "In fact, come

with me." She tapped the special conference media badge hanging around her neck. "I'll get you in."

"Thanks!" Maddie said. She took her brother's hand, and together they followed Nyota over to Ballroom A. No one looked twice at them when she led them inside.

When they took seats, Nyota whispered, *"I'll slip out now. This place is a goldmine for your father's show. Wall-to-wall wackos! You guys have fun, and we'll meet up again after the session."*

"You rule," Theo said.

She winked at him before heading off.

When Nyota was gone, Maddie looked to the front of the room. There was a screen that said, "Session A-1: The Aliens Among Us." The red-robed alien they'd seen greeting everyone at the cocktail party last night was standing at a podium next to it.

"Welcome! Welcome!" he said, as his fellow aliens settled into the seats. "My name is Wally. I am the President of Alien Nation, the organization that sponsors ET-Con. I wanted to run session A-1 because it's for newbies. I'm guessing you don't know much about extraterrestrials. Am I right?" Everyone in the room nodded their extraterrestrial heads. "After all, why else come to a basic introduction to the types of aliens on Earth? So, let's get started!"

He began showing slides depicting dozens of alien races. There were Andromedans, who looked like people but were larger and made of pure energy, and Little Green Men, which Maddie and Theo were surprised to learn was their actual species' name. They were, well, little and green, though both male and female. There were also Nordic aliens, who appeared to be super-tall alien supermodels; Reptilians, who looked like human/reptile crossbreeds; and Sirians, who were aquatic-looking humanoids. And many more.

When Wally was done, he asked if there were any questions.

Theo jumped to his feet with his hand raised and made that annoying, *"ooh, ooh, ooh"* noise that annoying kids made in class. Maddie turned and Eye-balled him a dire warning not to embarrass her. She looked around to make sure no one was filming him.

"Yes? In the back?"

"What kind of alien is J-Peg?"

Everyone in the room laughed.

"You mean J-*Rod,*" Wally said.

"You know what I meant!"

"Theo!" Maddie scolded, which made everyone laugh even more.

"J-Rod," Wally said, "is a Grey, a big-eyed, no-nosed, slit-mouthed alien — exactly like me!"

"Maybe you're him then!"

*"Theo!"*

Again, the room burst into laughter, but this time it lasted only a few seconds, because the door to the session room suddenly flew open, silencing everyone.

A Little Green Man alien, who was actually a rather tall woman, rushed inside. "J-Rod!" she cried.

"The *real* J-Rod that escaped from Area 51! It's true! It really *did* escape! It's hiding! But not in the desert! It's in disguise! *Here! At ET-Con!"*

CHAPTER TEN

# THE REAL AREA 51

The Yuck drove along smooth roads for about an hour, then bounced on secondary roads for about twenty minutes. Max, after eating a nutrition bar, spent his time looking at everything in the camper under his spy-nifying glass. And he couldn't help but peek out through the curtains on the Fifth Wheel's side windows every few minutes. Each time, he saw figures scampering through the sun-baked sagebrush. Some were dressed as aliens. Others, on the hunt, had those gigantic butterfly nets. One time he saw the second type chasing the first.

*"People,"* Max sighed.

Finally, the Yuck left the secondary roads for *really* bad paths, and it bounced crazily for a few minutes

before coming to a stop. Max dared to peek through the curtains again when the engine shut off. Outside was brown and barren. They seemed to be parked directly in front of a mountain.

In the middle of nowhere.

Max waited for a secret stone door to slide open. He'd never been so excited in his life.

But it didn't happen.

Instead, he saw a short man in a military uniform appear from behind a craggy outcrop in the mountainside. There were pins above his pockets and on his lapels and patches on his shoulders. He walked swiftly toward the Yuck and climbed inside.

*"A Colonel!"* Max whispered, amazed. He had a book about military ranks. He knew exactly which pile on his floor it was in, too. And how far down.

"Mr. Mattigan?" asked a voice over the walkie-talkie.

"Yes, sir. This is Kirk, my cameraman. I hope you don't mind him recording our conversation. It's for my show."

"That'll be fine. I am Colonel Mike Blanchard. If you don't mind, I'd like to talk here. It's best that you don't enter the facility, or even see how I left it, especially if you intend to film. I hope you understand that it's for your own protection. In fact, why don't we take a drive?"

"Of course," said Marcus. "Where shall we go?"

"Let's just head toward the city."

The Yuck started up. It turned around, and just like that, they were bouncing along again.

*dad's meeting a kernel in the yuck!*

*kernel blancherd!  IF that's his REAL name!*

*he came out of a secret mountain but we don't get to go in!*

"So, Mr. Mattigan," said Colonel Blanchard. "I imagine you have some thoughts. I'd love to hear them because — I assure you — there are no aliens in the custody of the United States government."

"Well, sir," Marcus replied, "I find that in these

sorts of cases, someone is always profiting. Further, I notice that these particular rumors are very well organized. Even though the viral videos of J-Rod hiding in the desert look amateur to my eye, they appear professionally amateur, if you take my meaning. And they hit the Web in all the right ways, at precisely the right times."

"You suspect some kind of publicity stunt."

"I do. I booked myself at the Circus Circus, where there's a convention going on. 'ET-Con,' it's called. Hundreds of goofballs running around dressed up like extraterrestrials. I wonder if an outfit like Alien Nation is capable of — "

Just then, Max heard ringing, so he grabbed his phone. But once again, it wasn't his phone. It was his dad's.

"Maddie?" Marcus said.

"Dad!" Maddie screamed. The phone was still on speaker.

"Maddie? *What's wrong?*"

*"Dad!"* Maddie screamed again, even louder this time. And she *had* to scream to be heard over the sounds of screaming in the background of wherever she was. "They say J-Rod is here! At the ET-Con! Everyone is running around trying to rip each other's costumes off to find it! It's total chaos! They cancelled the conference! You've got to get back here RIGHT NOW!"

CHAPTER ELEVEN

# TOTAL CHAOS

"Crikey," said Maddie, putting her phone away. "This is really not good."

"True story," said Theo, chewing a PB & B. "It's awesome."

"It's gold," said Nyota, scanning left and right with her camera. "Pure video *gold.*"

They were standing in the lobby of Circus Circus, watching a riot unfold around them. The kids' costumes had been ripped right off of them. Fortunately, they were wearing their jeans and T-shirts underneath. And since they looked like humans now, no one was interested in attacking them anymore.

But the still-aliens continued to attack each other, big time. Every sort described by Wally was there. They were all running around in circles, away from one another, but also at one another. At the same time, everyone was snapping pictures with their phones, trying to be the one to find J-Rod, or at least to capture his capture on camera.

Hotel security was trying to get control of the situation, but only sort of. Mostly, they were in on the madness, too, unless it was normal procedure to grab people by their faces. It was the most absurd scene Maddie and Theo had ever witnessed.

*"Aliens,"* they sighed.

"Look at that!" Theo cried.

"I know."

Incredibly, the zombies had not taken the slightest notice of the riot. They just kept pushing their buttons, rolling their dice, and moving their chips, exactly as if nothing insane was happening all around them.

*"Zombies,"* Maddie sighed.

"Huh?" said Theo.

Maddie's phone buzzed, so she took it back out. She and Theo looked at the display screen.

*publicity stunt! no real j-rod. on way back! driving fast!*

*dad's gonna bust those liars so bad!*

Maddie didn't know how to react to this. She just stood there. This news was terribly disappointing. There was no way around it. She was sad.

"What's a publicity stunt?" Theo asked. "Some kind of show?"

"It means it's all a fake, just to get attention."

"Can it be a publicity stunt *and* aliens?"

Maddie Eyeballed her little brother.

"Don't Teachable Moment me!" Theo snarled. "I have peanut butter AND banana in my sandwiches!" He held up what was left as proof.

Maddie didn't Teachable Moment her little brother. Instead, she said, "Theo Mattigan, you are a genius!"

"True story!" Theo cried. "I am?"

"Think about it. Let's say you're an alien who's been held by the government — for decades."

"Okay. I'm an alien who's been held by the government for decades."

"You're going to plan your escape very carefully."

"I'm going to plan my escape very carefully."

"Stop that. Look out!"

Theo ducked, just as a big little green alien threw a little little green alien right over his head and into a water feature. There was a huge splash, which Theo also ducked. But real police were finally arriving on the scene, which was a relief.

"I read about this J-Rod guy," Maddie said when it seemed safe to continue. "He wasn't, like, locked up in a cell and experimented on or anything like that. He was in charge of helping the government try to rebuild all the technology from his home planet."

"Okay," Theo replied.

"So, think about it. If you were planning to be an

alien on the loose in Las Vegas, wouldn't it be helpful if everyone was totally distracted, looking all over the place for you, even thinking everyone and their mother *was* you?"

"I guess so."

"And if you were really, super smart, where would be the very last place people would look for you?"

"At an alien convention?"

"Dressed up as — ?"

*"Yourself!"* Theo shrieked. "I WAS RIGHT! *Told* you I was right!"

"Then you would cause a riot, so that in all the chaos, you could quietly slip — "

"Look at that!"

"THEO, WILL YOU PLEASE STOP DOING THAT! *Oh*, I see!"

Theo was pointing out past the casino's front entrance. There, climbing into a limo, was Wally, still wearing his J-Rod mask and robes.

But the limo couldn't get out of the driveway,

because an unwieldy vehicle had just pulled up and accidentally blocked it in.

The Yuck!

## CHAPTER TWELVE

# UNMASKED

"Dad!" Maddie shouted into her phone. "Don't let that limo out! It's — it's — !" She didn't know what to tell him.

Maddie and Theo sprinted outside just as her father — along with both a man with a video camera and a military officer — climbed out of the Yuck. Police were now swarming into the casino. A group of them stopped at the military officer's request and surrounded the limo with guns drawn.

Guns!

The cops gestured for the passenger to get out, and moments later, Wally emerged, *still* in his J-Rod costume. "Whoa! *Whoa!*" he called, putting his hands up. "There's no need for violence!"

Nyota and Kirk were getting every bit of it on film.

In all the confusion, Max slipped out of the Fifth Wheel and rushed over to his brother and sister. "*There's* something you don't see every day," he said to them, taking in the wild scene.

Maddie hugged her brother, but quickly let him go. She was incredibly relieved to see him in one piece. Her stomach had stopped hurting at the sight of him, but it was starting up again as the cops approached Wally. A large crowd of people was gathering around.

"What?" Max asked.

"That really *is* J-Rod," Maddie told him. "We figured it out."

"*I* figured it out," Theo corrected.

"He's wearing a J-Rod mask *over* his J-Rod face," Maddie explained. "Dad's about to see that aliens are real."

"Wow."

"This is not good — really, really not good,"

Maddie insisted. "He's not ready for this! He still wants to believe that his father never had a good reason for leaving him! And — " She didn't even want to bring up their mother.

"You're probably right," Max agreed. "What can we do?"

The kids had no idea what to do, but their father seemed to. Marcus Mattigan did what he did best: unmask liars. He walked over to Wally and pulled the J-Rod mask right off his head, revealing — a very human face.

"Human mask!" Theo shouted. "Human mask under the J-Rod mask *over* the J-Rod face!"

Marcus heard his son, even over all the commotion, which was mostly a confused collection of shouts along the lines of "who the heck is that guy?" But he did not try to pull the man's skin off his skull.

Instead, he looked into Kirk and Nyota's cameras, which were now right up on him, and said, "I am Marcus Mattigan, professional skeptic and host of 'Monstrous Lies with Marcus Mattigan,' and this man, the host of ET-Con, is responsible for all the J-Rod nonsense. He is a fraud. There are no aliens being held by the US government. In fact, there are no aliens on Earth — and there never have been."

"Alright, alright!" Wally complained. "No need for cops! I'll explain! Yes, alright, I'll say it right into the cameras if it'll make you feel better. Let's get a close-up here. Good. Yes, yes, it's true. It's all been a PR stunt, and a darn good one, too, if I do say so myself. We're releasing a movie in a few months, called — Wait for it: "J-Rod!" Great title, am I right? The conference, the escape rumors and phony sightings — all part of the hype. Brand building, and all that. It's business, fellas! No need to get bent out of shape!"

The cops, bent out of shape or not, put Wally in cuffs.

"'Course I'll deny all this later and claim you made me say it!" Wally shouted as they led him away. "No! I'll say the aliens made me say it! I'm a genius! They're making me say that they're making me say it!"

The crowd, mostly made up of aliens in shredded costumes, seemed terribly let down. With shoulders sagging, they shuffled away.

Soon enough, the only people standing in front of Circus Circus were Kirk, Nyota, three Mattigan kids, their dad, and Colonel Mike Blanchard.

"Outstanding," the Colonel said. He put out his hand. Marcus took it, and they shook. "I'd like to thank you on behalf of the United States of America. I'm sure that unmasking will be all over the news within a few hours. Then, at least for a while, we'll have some peace and quiet around here."

"You're very welcome," Marcus said. "Do you need a ride — back?"

"Not necessary. I have some urgent business to attend to in town. May I ask what your plans are?"

"Oh, well — " Marcus looked at his kids and asked, "You guys done with rides and games?"

"We haven't ridded any rides or played any games!" Theo wailed.

"Theo!" Max and Maddie cried. "You mean you haven't ridden *enough* rides and games."

"You know what I meant!"

"Well, it looks like we'll be heading back home tomorrow morning," Marcus laughed. Then he thanked Kirk and Nyota, who promised to send him their footage first thing in the morning.

When Kirk and Nyota walked away, Marcus turned to shake hands with Mike Blanchard one more time, but the Colonel was already gone.

"Huh," Marcus said. "Duty calls, I guess. Well, gang. Let me go park the Yuck. Time to get our circus on, now that this Circus Circus circus is behind us. See what I did — *Hey, come back here, you rascals. I'm not clowning around!*"

## CHAPTER THIRTEEN

# FORCING IT A BIT

The Mattigans spent the rest of the day riding rides, wasting their money on unwinnable games (at least the ones that were actually games), and stuffing their faces with deliciously disgusting food.

They had a blast, especially Marcus, who had, within the hour, gotten word that his show was no longer on hold. But the truth was that the kids were forcing it a bit. They admitted it to one another on the Canyon Blaster coaster.

"I'm really happy for Dad," Maddie told her brothers. "I haven't seen him in this good a mood in — I don't know how long. But still — "

"I know," Max said. "We came for an alien. And I wanted to *help*, not just hide in a camper all day. I didn't use a single thing in my spy kit."

"But spy work can be horribly boring, right?" Maddie pointed out. "That's what people don't realize. You've told me that."

"Yeah," Max admitted, "but it's supposed to wind up with the spy *catching* somebody."

"I guess we can hardly expect to find a Mysterious Monster every time we go looking for one," Maddie had to admit. "What's bothering *you,* Theo?"

"I just want to go home."

"Really?" Maddie said. "I thought you wanted to stay here forever."

"Fine!" Theo snapped. "I wanted my Bigfoot to have a friend! *Okay?"*

Maddie and Max smiled at each other just as the coaster car was about to plummet down the steepest slope.

All three Mattigans put their arms up and screamed.

## CHAPTER FOURTEEN

# UP TO SOMETHING

At nine o'clock the next morning, the Yuck pulled out of the Circus Circus parking lot with four Mattigans buckled in.

"That went rather well, don't you think?" Marcus asked his kids, all of whom had already taken out their phones. "I mean, it really couldn't have been easier. In fact, I've never had an investigation go so smoothly in all — "

"Dad," Max suddenly interrupted, putting his phone down. "Did you know, even though you said we weren't when we got it, that we *are* actually allowed to ride in the Fifth Wheel in Oregon, as long as communication is possible with the driver?"

"Really?" Marcus said. "Well, I suppose we could

use the walkie-talkies. How about in Nevada?"

"Um — "

Maddie turned around and looked at Max. She didn't Eyeball him, though. She was curious. He was up to something.

"I think maybe it's the same," Max said. *Omelet*, he mouthed to his sister.

"And you'd like to ride back there?"

"Yeah. I think it'd be fun. Just for a little while."

"I do, too," Maddie said. "I didn't sleep very well on that couch. I'd love to take a short nap. You know what I'm like when I don't get enough sleep."

"That's a winning argument if I ever heard one," Marcus admitted. "Theo?" he said, "I suppose you want to abandon me, too?"

"Yes, way!"

"Theo!" Maddie cried, for what felt like the millionth time.

"Don't worry, buddy," Marcus told him. "I know what you meant."

"Told ya!"

Marcus pulled the Yuck over since they hadn't gotten on the highway yet and let the kids go back into the camper.

"All aboard," Max said into the walkie-talkie after they'd chosen seats. "Ready to launch. Over."

"Roger that," Marcus replied. "Houston, we *don't* have a problem."

"Except with your sense of humor. We see what you did there. Over."

## CHAPTER FIFTEEN

# FIFTH WHEEL, PART II

"It was too easy," Max said.

"What do you mean?" Maddie asked.

"The job! It was too easy! Something isn't right. It's like Dad always says: if it sounds too good to be true, it probably is."

"Maybe you're right," Maddie allowed. "In fact, something tells me you *are* right. What exactly happened yesterday? Tell us everything you remember. Tell it back like a spy."

"Alright. Good idea," Max agreed. "Okay. So, Dad came in with that Kirk guy and ate — omelets! — and made a call. To an Air Base, I think. He said who he was and what he was doing. But he had to leave a message. Then they went up to the Yuck. But then he got a call up there, on his cell."

"They called him back."

"I guess so. Well, he said, 'Thanks for calling me back so fast,' or something like that. But now that I think about it, he said they were probably not going to call him back. That's why they were driving to the base."

"Did you actually hear them say, 'We're returning your call'?"

*"Hmmm."*

"Think."

"No, I don't think they did. Actually, they didn't. I'm sure of it."

"Okay, then what?"

"It was Colonel Blanchard, and he said he thought Dad could help, and that he would send him some GPS coordinates, but that they wouldn't take him to where most people thought Area 51 was."

"I guess that kind of makes sense."

"And then we drove to the middle of nowhere. To a mountain. And Colonel Blanchard came out of it and got into the Yuck."

"Wait a minute. Did you actually *see* him come out of the mountain?"

"Well, no."

*"Hmmm."*

"Maybe *he's* the J-Rod!" Theo said.

"Sure, why not!" Max allowed, halfway serious and halfway joking. "Maybe he'd been waiting for an opportunity to escape for a long time, and then there's all these crazy rumors, which maybe he started, and there's all these phony J-Rods running around in the desert, so he figured he'd be sort of safe out there." Max was getting warmed up, talking faster as he went. "But he knew he'd need a way *out* of the desert, so he lured Dad out there to get him. And he knew Dad was coming to Nevada, because of his press release! But of course he wouldn't lure him out to the *real* Area 51, but instead to some random nowhere spot where he was hiding. *Then* — after Dad does the job of calming down all the rumors about escaped aliens, he would — Well, he would still need to get out of the larger area, so — so he would — "

Max got up and walked to the closet he'd hidden in just yesterday, and he finished his speech by saying, "He would sneak into our Fifth Wheel and have us drive him out of Nevada. Ah-*ha!*" he shouted, just for the fun of it, throwing open the door with the flourish of a magician.

And there, in the closet, stood a cowering Colonel Mike Blanchard.

## CHAPTER SIXTEEN

# ROADBLOCK

After a moment of stunned silence, Marcus's voice came over the walkie-talkie. "Kids," he said, sounding concerned. "There's a roadblock of some kind. Lots of police. I'm sure it's nothing to worry about." The Yuck slowed down and stopped.

*"Please,"* begged Colonel Mike Blanchard. *"Please, hide me."*

Maddie and Max were still too shocked that Max's story had turned out to be correct to do anything at all, so Theo got up and closed the closet door.

Moments later, the door to the Fifth Wheel opened to reveal their father and a hulking police officer. The officer looked rather unhappy to see the kids.

"Sir," he said to Marcus, "are you aware that it's against the law in the state of Nevada to have passengers riding back here?"

"Uh, well," Marcus said, "I understand that, in Oregon, it's legal as long as communication is available with the driver. We're using walkie-talkies."

Max held up their walkie-talkie as proof.

"I did notice the Oregon plates," the officer said, stepping up into the camper. The kids Eyeballed each other, trying not to look at one particular closet — and to avoid having three giant meltdowns, right then and there.

"What's the holdup?" Theo demanded, and way too loudly.

*"Theo!"* his brother and sister hissed.

"You know what I meant!"

Luckily, the officer thought this was funny. "It's fine," he said. "Escaped prisoner from a local detention center. I need to do a quick search for your own safety. You never know."

Now the kids started to sweat. Their knees started to shake, too, so they all sat down. When the officer stepped into the bathroom, they traded desperate glances, willing each other to do something.

The officer came out of the bathroom. He got on his hands and knees and looked under the bunks. Then he got up and started opening closets. When he reached the last one, all three kids were just about to scream, *"Nooo!"*

But he didn't open it.

"Wait a minute," the officer said, looking at the poster on the door. He turned and asked, "Are you Marcus Mattigan — the professional skeptic?"

"I am, yes."

"I saw you on the news last night! You were great!" The officer moved away from the closet to shake Marcus's hand. "You've done law enforcement around here a real solid. The Alien Nation is clearing out of town."

"I'm so glad I was able to help."

"I don't think we have anything to worry about here," the officer decided. "I'll move along. Don't worry about the kids riding in the camper. You'll be back in Oregon soon enough."

"Well, great, then. Thanks!"

The officer climbed out of the Fifth Wheel. Before Marcus followed, he turned to the kids, and said, "You guys okay?" His children were all still white as ghosts, but also looking strangely elated.

"All good!" they promised.

"Outlaws, the bunch of you," Marcus said. But he winked to show them he was kidding.

And then, to their incredible relief, he climbed out of the camper, too.

## CHAPTER SEVENTEEN

# J-ROD

The kids rushed to the closet and opened it again. There, still cringing, was Colonel Mike Blanchard.

"It's okay," Max said. "You can come out. They were looking for you, but it's safe now. Your plan worked perfectly."

The Colonel stepped gingerly out of the closet. Without saying a word, he sat down on one of the padded chairs and let out a sigh that must have been filling his entire body. The kids took seats, as well.

"How do you know they were looking for him?" Maddie asked Max. "The officer said they were looking for an escaped prisoner."

"Of course, they were looking for him," Max

said. "Don't you think they know he escaped?"

"Well, yeah. I guess so."

"And now we know why he picked Dad to smuggle him out of Nevada. Who is the last person on Earth the authorities would think is stashing an alien in his Fifth Wheel?"

"Marcus Mattigan, professional skeptic!" Maddie said, amazed. "He stopped searching the second he realized who Dad was. Max, you're a genius!"

"Spynius."

"Um — no."

"Can we see your Martian face?"

*"Theo!"* Maddie was horrified. "That's incredibly rude!"

"And Martians are from Mars," Max said. "You have no idea where he — "

"YOU KNOW WHAT I MEANT!"

"Hold on a moment," Colonel Blanchard said. Then he leaned over and put his hands under his shirt collar. Then, in one swift motion, he appeared to rip off his face.

It was a mask. A remarkable human mask.

And then, there he was, sitting right in front of Maddie, Max and Theo Mattigan: J-Rod. His real face looked pretty much exactly like the J-Rod masks: large almond eyes, slitty mouth, no nose to speak of.

The Mattigans, polite as they were (two-thirds of them, anyway), couldn't help themselves: they jumped right out of their chairs and backed away from the alien.

Then J-Rod pulled off his hands. He had fake hands over his alien hands, which turned out to look a lot like human hands, except he only had four fingers on each.

No one spoke a word for a solid minute.

*"Are* you from Mars?" Theo finally asked.

"I don't know," J-Rod said, and he sounded sad. "I don't know whether I come from another planet, or whether I am a human from the far future. Or maybe there's another story altogether that explains me."

"How can that be?" Maddie asked. This was completely unexpected. He seemed harmless, and she was feeling terrible about having leapt up like that. Her stomach was suddenly hurting exactly the way it did when she lied. She went and sat down, and after she Eyeballed them, her brothers did, too.

"I was a baby on board the ship that crashed here on Earth," J-Rod explained. "There were no others. I was raised by your government, in secret. I have tried my best to help them learn the technology that brought me here, but for the most part, I have failed. For me, as for them, it is too complicated."

"Have there been other — ships?" Maddie asked.

"No," J-Rod said. "All fakes and frauds. Every one of them. Which is why your government will not wish to lose track of me. But I've decided that I want to live my own life. Actually, I'd like to put my time and energy into finding where I came from, into finding others like me — my parents, if that's possible."

"We can help," Maddie declared. She didn't decide to say that. She just said it. And she could see by the look on her brothers' faces that they agreed completely.

"You can?" J-Rod asked.

"Do you mind a roommate?" Max asked.

"Do you mind a pet?" Theo asked.

"Do you mind a roommate that *is* a pet?" Maddie and Max asked at the exact same time. They laughed.

"You are an interesting family," J-Rod said, smiling hopefully.

"True story!"

"Houston, do you copy?" Marcus asked over the walkie-talkie. "You all getting along back there?"

"Notta foot!"

"Notta fist!"

"Notta finger!"

"Notta little green antinna, either!" Theo added.

*"Antenna,"* his brother and sister corrected.

"YOU KNOW WHAT I MEANT!"

# POSTSCRIPT

# ALIEN

And that, dear readers, is how what happened in Vegas *got out of* Vegas.

Bet you didn't see that coming.

But I hope you *were* betting on the Mattigans (not your allowance, of course). They may be *out there*, but they're doing the best they can, traveling through unmapped territory in a world where not everything is as it seems.

Some people call that trip *Life*.

Discuss among yourselves.

Meanwhile, I'll get started sinking my teeth into the next Mattigan adventure.

It's a bloody good one.

Here's some advice for *your* trip: Keep your campers unlocked, and don't stop leaving those Martian-mallows under the bunks. (See what I did there?)

Sincerely,

Your pal

## About The Author

David Michael Slater is an acclaimed author of books for children, teens, and adults. His work for children includes the picture books *Cheese Louise!, The Bored Book*, and *The Boy & the Book*, as  well as the on-going teen fantasy series, *Forbidden Books*, which is being developed for film by a former producer of *The Lion King*. David's work for adults includes the hilarious comic-drama, *Fun & Games*, which the New York Journal of Books writes "works brilliantly." David teaches in Reno, Nevada, where he lives with his wife and son. You can learn more about David and his work at www.davidmichaelslater.com.

## About Mysterious Monsters

Mysterious Monsters is a humorous six-book early chapter book series full of mystery and adventure. When Marcus Mattigan, star of the popular show "Monstrous Lies with Marcus Mattigan" offers to let his kids, Maddie, Max, and Theo, travel around the country with him as he exposes frauds and fakes, the trio manages to find and capture the world's most mysterious and elusive creatures — and then to hide them in their increasingly crowded basement. As you can imagine, with each book, the situation gets more and more hairy.

# Credits

This book is a work of art produced by Incorgnito Publishing Press.

Susan Comninos
*Editor*

Mauro Sorghienti
*Illustrator/Artist*

Star Foos
*Designer*

Janice Bini
*Chief Reader*

Daria Lacy
*Graphic Production*

Michael Conant
*Publisher*

March 2018
*Incorgnito Publishing Press*

CPSIA information can be obtained
at www.ICGtesting.com
Printed in the USA
LVOW10s0348130218
566347LV00001B/1/P